This edition published by Parragon Books Ltd in 2014

Parragon Books Ltd
Chartist House
15–17 Trim Street
Bath BA1 1HA, UK
www.parragon.com

ISBN 978-1-4723-7983-2

Printed in China

Bath • New York • Cologne • Melbourne • Delhi
Hong Kong • Shenzhen • Singapore • Amsterdam

Dusty was a small-town crop-dusting plane with a big dream. He wanted to race in the Wings Around The Globe Rally with the fastest planes in the world. He loved racing so much he even daydreamed about it – especially when he was working!

Dusty's best friend was a fuel truck named Chug. He gave Dusty instructions over a radio to help Dusty practise for the rally. Eventually, though, Chug decided Dusty needed someone who knew more about flying to train him.

He suggested Skipper, a grumpy old navy war hero. Skipper wouldn't fly anymore, though. Sparky the tug pushed him wherever he wanted to go.

When Dusty got the courage to ask Skipper to coach him, Skipper refused.

Dusty kept training, and finally he went to fly in the qualifying race for the Wings Around The Globe Rally. The most famous racer, Ripslinger, laughed at Dusty. So did the crowd. They thought it was ridiculous to let a crop duster into the race!

Dusty raced well, but not well enough to get a place in the rally. He sadly went back to his home town of Propwash Junction.

One day soon after, an official from the race came
to town with good news. Dusty could join the rally,
after all! Suddenly, Dusty began to wonder if he was
good enough to compete in such a difficult race.

Skipper finally agreed to train Dusty, but he noticed the little plane didn't want to fly high.

Skipper wanted to know why. After making excuses, Dusty finally confessed his big secret: he was afraid of heights!

Skipper had an idea. He had Dusty race the shadow of a passenger plane that flew over Propwash Junction every day. That way, Dusty could practise racing without flying too high. Dusty worked hard. Soon Skipper told him he was ready for the rally.

Dusty flew to New York to join the other racers for the start of the event. He was disappointed when racing stars Ripslinger and Bulldog weren't friendly to him. He liked Ishani, though. She was nice!

El Chupacabra, the racer from Mexico, made an exciting entrance. He was a superstar in his country. Dusty was thrilled to meet him!

The Wings Around The Globe Rally had several
stages. During the first part, the racers flew over
the Atlantic Ocean. Dusty flew low, got caught in a
freezing hailstorm and almost crashed! He came in
last place.

During the next stage, Dusty heard some calls for help over his radio. Bulldog was in trouble! The British plane had an oil spill that made it impossible for him to see. Dusty flew next to him and helped him land. Now Bulldog was proud to be Dusty's friend.

Dusty was still in last place, but soon he started moving up in the rankings. He was becoming an international star – Ripslinger didn't like that.

Dusty's friends back home watched it all on TV. They radioed Dusty at every stop. Skipper gave him advice for each new stage of the race. He knew about all kinds of flying conditions from his navy missions.

The next stage was over the Pacific Ocean, so Skipper warned Dusty to be careful of storms.

Then Dusty learned that all his friends would be meeting him when he landed in Mexico. He couldn't wait!

The next morning, one of Ripslinger's sidekicks flew past Dusty and broke off his antenna! Without his antenna, Dusty soon became lost and his fuel ran low. Luckily, two navy fighter jets rescued him and took him to the *Dwight D. Flysenhower* – Skipper's old navy aircraft carrier.

Fuelled up and with a new antenna, Dusty was heading to Mexico when a storm hit. He had to be rescued by the Mexican Navy.

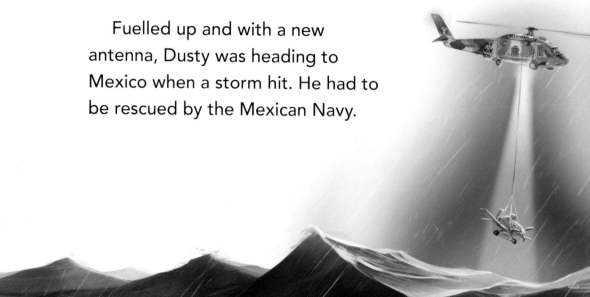

When he got to Mexico, Dusty was in such bad shape, it was clear he couldn't fly the last part of the rally. To make things worse, he had discovered that Skipper had never been a war hero. Dusty couldn't believe that Skipper had lied to him. Dusty felt sad – and angry!

Then Dusty got an amazing surprise. The other racers arrived with new parts for him. Now he could be repaired and finish the rally!

The next morning, Dusty took off for New York, determined to win. Once again, Ripslinger and his teammates tried to knock him out of the race.

Then Skipper appeared! It was the first time Dusty had ever seen him fly! Skipper stopped Ripslinger's team from hurting Dusty again.

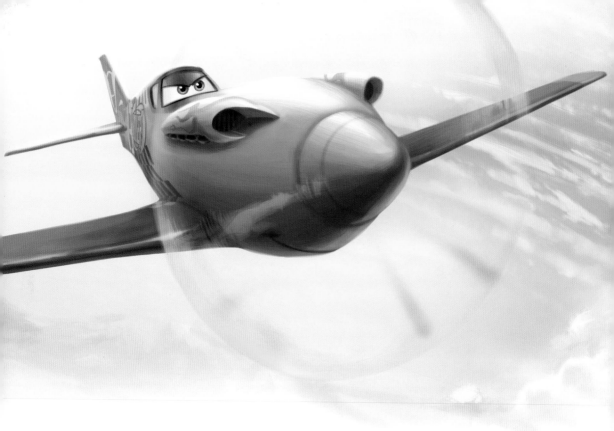

Ripslinger raced ahead.

"Go get him!" said Skipper.

This time, Dusty faced his fear of heights.
He soared high in the sky, way above the clouds.
It worked! With the tailwinds behind him, he easily
caught up to Ripslinger.

When they reached the finish line, Dusty swerved past Ripslinger – and won!

Dusty's pals were so proud of him and he was grateful for their help. But Dusty's biggest thanks went to Skipper. He had coached Dusty to victory and was still his hero, no matter what.